Read Me to Sleep™

How to use this story to help ease your child to sleep

1 **PREPARE.** After reading these instructions and before reading to your child, listen to a sample of the story being read aloud at this link: **www.readmetosleepbooks.com**. Follow along with the text and notice the pace, the pauses, and the emphasis on certain words, as well as the extended vowel sounds. You may want to read the text aloud by yourself at first to ensure the extended vowel sounds and unnaturally slow reading pace become comfortable. After practicing several times, you may want to adapt word emphasis to fit your own rhythms.

2 **SHARE.** When you're ready for a nighttime reading, let your child browse through the book and enjoy the pictures first, so he or she can imagine them as you read the story aloud. This should be the last story read at bedtime; it is encouraged that you read other favorite lap time or bedtime stories prior to this book. At this point in your bedtime routine, your child should be ready to relax in a resting position and close his or her eyes.

3 **RELAX AND BREATHE.** Before you start the story, take several deep, cleansing breaths and encourage your child to do so along with you. Breathing is a key relaxation technique used in Read Me to Sleep. It's recommended to inhale through the nose and exhale through the mouth audibly, with the exhalation twice as long as the inhalation. This will force you and your child to take deeper, calming breaths.

4 **READ THE STORY ALOUD** in a slow, gentle voice, following the reading cues suggested:
- You may choose to replace the **green** words with objects (or people) from your child's life that are meaningful and provide comfort.
- When you encounter **blue** words, stretch out the primary vowel sound in each word.
- Read the **purple** words in a hushed voice or a whisper.
- Line breaks demonstrate where you should pause briefly, with ellipses demonstrating a longer pause.

5 **RETURN TO THE BEGINNING** if your child is not asleep by the end of the story. Simply maintain your rhythm and begin the text again without alerting the child that the story has ended; the repetition and cyclical pattern are calming, and the story should feel like an endless entry into sleep.

Little, Brown and Company

Hachette Book Group
1290 Avenue of the Americas, New York, NY 10104
Visit us at lb-kids.com

Little, Brown and Company is a division of Hachette Book Group, Inc.
The Little, Brown name and logo are trademarks of Hachette Book Group, Inc.

The publisher is not responsible for websites (or their content) that are not owned by the publisher.

First Edition: April 2016

Library of Congress Cataloging-in-Publication Data
Names: Reade, Maisie, author. | Huliska-Beith, Laura, 1964- illustrator.
Title: Let's go to sleep / by Maisie Reade ; illustrated by Laura Huliska-Beith.
Other titles: Let us go to sleep
Description: First edition. | New York : Little, Brown and Company, 2016. | Series: Read me to sleep | Summary: "In a story designed to lull children to sleep with a variety of breathing and relaxation exercises, Mama Bird leads a journey to the magical Forest of Dreams." —Provided by publisher.
Identifiers: LCCN 2015040180 | ISBN 9780316356558 (hardcover)
Subjects: | CYAC: Bedtime—Fiction. | Relaxation—Fiction.
Classification: LCC PZ7.1.A434 Le 2016 | DDC [E]—dc23
LC record available at http://lccn.loc.gov/2015040180

10 9 8 7 6 5 4 3 2 1

PHX

PRINTED IN THE UNITED STATES OF AMERICA

Read Me to Sleep™

Let's Go to Sleep

By Maisie Reade

Illustrated by Laura Huliska-Beith

Little, Brown and Company

New York   Boston

Take my hand, little child,
and follow this winding path
to the Forest of Dreams.
Here the air is magic
that you breathe in…
and breathe out.
It fills every part of you with your very best dreams
that send you right to sleep with a smile.
The way is lit by warmly glowing fireflies,
and a gentle breeze carries a scent of pine
that you breathe in…
and breathe out.

Before you can say "sleepytime," you've arrived!
See? You're surrounded by all of your friends,
like Little Fawn and Tiny Squirrel
and Cozy Bear and even Lazy Lion.
They're on the very same journey that you are…
the journey to dreamland.

Mama Bird welcomes you to the Forest of Dreams.
"Take off your shoes and get cozy.
You'll be here awhile," she tells you.
Go ahead…
The ground is cool and soft on your bare feet
like a sandy beach at twilight,
and your toes sink in just right.

Then, Mama Bird tells you a very important secret:
If you know how to breathe,
you know how to sleep.
It's true! If you know how to breathe,
you know how to sleep.
After the word "sleep," inhale and push a complete breath out through the mouth.

Mama Bird is the only animal in this forest
who stays awake through the dawn.
She watches over the others all night long,
and is always sure that they're safe.

When you encounter blue words, stretch out the primary vowel sound. The words in purple can be said in a hushed voice or a whisper.

Little Fawn is here, too, but Little Fawn isn't sure what to do.
She thinks she needs *things* to put her to sleep.
Little Fawn says,

"Mama Bird, I'm here, and I'm ready for sleep.
Mama Bird, can you bring my warm, furry blankie?
Mama Bird, can you bring my fluffiest pillow?
Mama Bird, can you bring my favorite little sparrow,
so I may hear her sweet songs?
Mama Bird, can you bring my softly glowing night-light?
I am so tired, so very tired.
I am ready for sleep…
so ready for sleep."

Take a deep breath in and exhale audibly before turning the page.

Mama Bird nods, and says,
"You could climb on my back
and we could look for your blankie.
We could fly high and low, to the tips of the treetops…
then dip down below—sailing into the hollows…
into burrows and tree nooks and nests."

Little Fawn gives a yawn.
"I'd like that," she responds.
Ready to fly, she trots over to Mama Bird.

Mama Bird shakes her head with a smile.
"We could look for your blankie, Little Fawn,
but you don't need your blankie…you don't need it at all.
The air in this forest is all that you need.
It's everywhere around you…
and everywhere inside you.
It's filled with magic that allows you to sleep.
So breathe deep and dream, Little Fawn,
breathe deep and dream!"

Mama Bird flutters her wings,
encouraging Little Fawn to come to rest.
"First you lie down, then close your eyes," she says.
"Take a long breath in and count to three…
so the air reaches all the way to your toes!
There it goes!

You may choose to prompt your child here by adding: "Breathe in…1…2…3…!"

"Hold your breath so it stays inside—just a few more seconds,
so your whole body is ready to fall asleep.
When you feel the magic tingle on the tips of your toes,
let out your breath, Little Fawn, until there's nothing left."

You may choose to prompt your child here by exhaling audibly with a "whoosh" sound for a count of six: "Whoooooooooosssssssh!"

Tiny Squirrel is still awake and scampers over.
Mama Bird tucks the little creature under her soft wing, and says,
"Let's breathe in together now, with all of your friends,
so we can help Tiny Squirrel fall asleep, too."

Now encourage your child to breathe in, hold the breath, and
breathe out along with you, as described on the first page.

Little Fawn **gives a** yawn.
"**You're right, Mama Bird. I don't need my** blankie.
Can we find my fluffiest pillow **instead?**
I am so tired, so **very tired.**
I am ready for sleep…
so **ready for** sleep."

Mama Bird nods, and says,
"**You could climb on my back and we could look for your** pillow.
We could fly here **and** there—**to mountains and peaks,**
to valleys and rivers, and soar far **over meadows**
into caves and canyons and dens."

Another yawn **from** Little Fawn.
"**What an adventure!**" **She** sighs. "**I'd love to go.**"

You may yawn and sigh along with Little Fawn. When you encounter blue *words, stretch out the primary vowel sound. You may also choose to* replace *"blankie" and "pillow" with other comforting objects from your child's world. The words in* purple *can be said in a hushed voice or a whisper.*

You may choose to incorporate the interactive breathing into the story, as shown in the notes below, or wait until the bottom of the page to breathe together.

Mama Bird shakes her head with a smile.
"Oh, but you don't need your pillow…you don't need it at all.
The air in this forest is all that you need.
It's everywhere around you, and everywhere inside you.
It's filled with magic that allows you to sleep.
If there's one thing you need, you need to breathe deep.
Take a long breath in and count to two,
so your belly inflates, just like a balloon!
You may choose to prompt your child here by adding: "Breathe in…1…2!"

"Now hold your breath so it stays inside—just a few more seconds,
so you feel the magic swirl right up to your heart.
Then let out your breath, Little Fawn, until there's nothing left."
You may choose to prompt your child here by exhaling audibly with a "whoosh" sound for a count of five: "Whoooooooooosssssssh!"

Cozy Bear is still awake and lumbers over for a hug.
Mama Bird's wings are open so wide,
they reach all the way around the drowsy cub.
"Let's breathe in together now, with all of your friends,
so we can help Cozy Bear fall asleep, too."

Now encourage your child to breathe in, hold the breath, and breathe out along with you, as described on the first page.

Little Fawn's **eyes start to fall shut.**
"You're right, Mama Bird. I don't need my blankie **or my** pillow.
But can we look for my favorite **little** sparrow,
so I may hear her sweet songs?
I am so tired, **so very** tired.
I am ready for sleep…so **ready for** sleep."

Mama Bird nods, and says,
"You could climb on my back
and we could look for your sparrow.
We could search far **and wide…**beyond **the wood's edge,**
over **the ocean, then** touch the horizon
to the north, and the south, and the east, and the west."

Little Fawn **opens one eye.**
"Yes, let's!" she says with a sigh. **"I'd love to go."**

Mama Bird shakes her head with a smile.
"Oh, but you don't need **your little** sparrow…**you don't need her at all.**
The air **in this forest is all that you need.**
It's every**where around you, and** every**where inside you.**
It's filled with magic **that allows you to sleep.**
So breathe **deep and dream,** Little Fawn,
breathe deep and dream!

"Take a long breath in
so the air can reach all the way to your fingertips.

You may choose to prompt your child here by adding: "Breathe in deep!"

"Hold your breath so it stays inside—just one more second,
so your fingers are tingly, and ready to sleep.
Then push out your breath, Little Fawn, until there's nothing left.
Keep going, keep going…"

You may choose to prompt your child here by exhaling audibly with a "whoosh" sound for a count of four: "Whooooooooooosssssssh!"

Lazy Lion is here, too, and she rolls over on her back for a belly rub.
Mama Bird tickles her tummy with the tips of her wings, and says,
"Let's breathe in together now, with all of your friends,
so we can help Lazy Lion fall asleep, too."

Now encourage your child to breathe in, hold the breath, and breathe out along with you, as described on the first page.

Little Fawn gives a yawn.
"You're right, Mama Bird.
I don't need my blankie, my pillow, or even my little sparrow.
But can we look for my night-light? Or maybe the moon?
I am so tired, so very tired.
I am ready for sleep…
so ready for sleep."

Mama Bird nods, and says,
"You could climb on my back and we could look for the moon.
We could fly to the clouds…and even to space.
We could sail past the sun and the planets and stars
and then we could make our way home."

Little Fawn is almost asleep now, but she knows the secret.
"We'll come home because I don't need light tonight.
I don't need it at all.
The air in this forest is all that I need.
It's everywhere around me
and everywhere inside me.
It's filled with magic that allows me to sleep.
If there's one thing I need, I need to breathe deep."

You may yawn along with Little Fawn. You may choose to replace "blankie," "pillow," "sparrow," and "night-light" with other comforting objects or pets from your child's world. When you encounter blue words, stretch out the primary vowel sound. The words in purple can be said in a hushed voice or a whisper.

When you encounter blue words, stretch out the primary vowel sound. The words in purple can be said in a hushed voice or a whisper.

Mama Bird smiles and nods.
"You're right, Little Fawn.
You don't need your blankie or your pillow,
your little sparrow or your night-light or even the moon.
You're so very tired; you're ready for sleep.
You want to go to sleep!

"Take one more breath in
so the air fills you all the way up…
from your toes to your belly to your heart…
then out to your fingers and up to your head!
When you feel the magic tingle all the way to your hair,
push out your breath, Little Fawn, until there's nothing left.
Whooooooooooossssssssh!"

If your child is still fully awake, he or she can now be prompted to breathe in, hold the breath, and breathe out along with you, as described on the first page.

And when you enter dreamland, dear child,
there is no better place to be tucked in
than the Forest of Dreams,
where Little Fawn and Tiny Squirrel, Cozy Bear and Lazy Lion,
and all of the other creatures are curled up tight...
and Mama Bird is awake all night watching over every creature,
making sure they are comfy, making sure they are safe.
Tomorrow night there will be a new little creature in the forest,
and you'll know exactly what to tell her, won't you?

You'll say,
"Take my hand, my friend,
and follow this winding path
to the Forest of Dreams.
Here the air is magic
that you breathe in...
and breathe out.
It fills every part of you with your very best dreams
that send you right to sleep with a smile."

Breathe deep and dream, my friends,
breathe deep and dream!

Return to the beginning if your child is not yet asleep.